DEITY

HARD TIME, BOOK 6

EREC STEBBINS

TWICE PI PRESS

Only one thing is impossible for God: to find any sense in any copyright law on the planet.—Mark Twain

This book is a work of fiction. Any references to historical events, real people, or real locales are used fictitiously. Other names, characters, places, and incidents are the product of the author's imagination, and any resemblance to actual events or locales or persons, living or dead, is entirely coincidental.

Content Guide

This novel contains depictions and references to events and ideas that some will find disturbing, possibly including, but not limited to, monsters, gore, death, torture, captivity, severe illness, pain, fear, medical procedures, and violence. There is also profanity and strong language, the challenging of some accepted norms, and the questioning of different kinds of authority, religious and secular. The book may also contain religion, Oxford commas, and an unnecessary number of tpyos and, grammer misteaks. Readers are asked to prepare accordingly.

1

ASLEEP

The fragment of masonry clanged off the metallic structure and plunged to the ground. It shattered with a puff of dust.

"Nice shot, Mateo!"

A gaunt teen grinned at his cheering friend. Piercings studded his face. Black hair dyed a rainbow of colors and shorn bald on the sides ran to the middle of his back. He hoisted another chipped brick.

Light faded through the grimed glass in the school hallways. The boys stood alone in the deserted corridors. They glared across a reflective, wet surface at a mechanical manikin mopping the floor.

The robot stuttered to a halt, reached down, and

grasped the broken pieces of stone in jointed, metallic fingers. Its camera-lens eyes clicked, focusing on the teens.

"Please place waste in the proper receptacles."

The voice was awkward, mocking human speech and uncanny in its near misses. The pair laughed.

"Remember," chirped the machine, "a clean school is a happy school."

"Fuck you, synth shit!"

With a loud grunt, the boy flung the piece. This larger fragment struck the bot at a knee joint, breaking the part. The right leg failed.

Mop launched skyward, arms flailing like a puppet with severed strings, the automaton plunged to the ground. Its head struck exposed piping. The right eye popped out, the lens shattering. Wires dangled from the bot's head, fixed to a naked camera circuit board.

Mateo whooped and pumped a fist.

"Hell, yeah!"

"Always be considerate to others. Vandalism is a crime."

Steam shot from the busted pipe and bathed the head of the robot, its words garbled in the noise.

Mateo bent down and raised a large slab of rock.

His companion grabbed his shoulder, a gray hoodie obscuring his features.

"Stop, man! That's enough. Let's get out of here!"

"I'm gonna wreck that thing, Dan," said Mateo, struggling as he lugged the large object toward the babbling bot.

Dan shook his head. "Why? We're gonna get caught!"

The android thrashed, words pouring out, the circuitry overheated.

"Fucking janibots," gasped Mateo. He stopped near the malfunctioning machine. "My dad started quark when these things took his job. My whole hood's outta work. These metal shits are takin' over everything."

The artificial voice croaked through the hissing steam.

"I am broken. Please return me to an authorized repair shop."

"Go to hell!"

Mateo heaved the heavy rock over his head. A metallic arm rose in defense. The boy dropped the slab over the janibot. The steam pipe bent back, angling the belching vapor. The rock smashed the metal skull of the robot, sparks spraying out like fireworks.

The janibot did not move.

"Okay, *now* we go?" begged Dan.

"Stop! Stop!"

The Woman placed her hands to her head, her eyes pinched closed. She swayed and fell to her knees.

Opening her eyes, she squinted, shaking her head.

"Where am I?"

The desert was gone. The mauled forms of Trunes and humans, of Fenn the Synth, gone. She floated in a multicolored nebula, rotating around a central point.

At that nexus burned a figure of dust and light. Humanoid with naked skin colored ash-gray and cracked like a field of aged volcanic rock. Light and dust squeezed between the deep fissures that opened to cosmic vistas.

"I am," said the Deity.

"What are you doing to me?" she shrieked, her eyes wide.

"Teaching."

The swirling gases of the nebula vanished and she stood beneath two teens glancing down at her.

Mateo sneered.

"Can't just leave it here."

Two hands reached toward her and grasped a body she could not feel. The grating sound of dragged metal tore through the echoing hallway. Her perspective shifted.

"God, this thing's heavy," gulped Mateo. "Stop staring and help!"

Another pair of arms reached toward her. A scraping rend reverberated through her teeth. She watched the ceiling move.

I'm moving. What am I?

The frame of a doorway. Fluorescent lighting replaced by a dim gray of an overcast sky. Above her, the red and straining faces of two adolescents.

"Now, the hard part," said Mateo.

Dan sighed. "Too high. We can't get it in there."

"Metal recycling. It'll get pounded. Scrapped. Justice."

"Jesus, Mateo. It's just a fucking janibot. Not like it's a real Synth or nothing. Ain't got no brains."

"It's got brains enough to take our lives away. Lift!"

The ground disappeared. A metal wall approached. Her vision spun as she fell. A dumpster, the ground, and then the sky as she landed in a vat of scrap.

"Truck comes tonight," said Mateo. "Teachers won't even know what happened to it."

"Cameras, duh?"

Mateo smirked. "Ain't been no money for years. Half don't work. I score Dream in that hall. Never been busted."

A hand reached up and yanked a lever. Darkness fell as a metal crash rang in her mind.

She lay inside the dark bin for hours. Or days. She could not tell. Displaced and projected, her sense of time crumbled. At last, the lid opened, but not to the recycling services.

The bright streetlamp LEDs backlit two figures. Their hair was long and full, flirting with translucent, faces obscured in shadow. One reached out a hand, thin filaments worming from the fingers and approaching her.

The worms are so warm.

The other Synth behind spoke. "We passed into a restricted zone. All communications must be verbal. Electromagnetic could be detected by any roving monitors and a violation recorded."

The near one retracted its hand and nodded. "Early quartz coupling model. Subminds are simple and poorly integrated. High probability that consciousness is below the treaty threshold."

"Do we need a more thorough scan?"

"Not here. My modules are current. New sensitivity. Sentience Rights will not apply."

"Then we are fortunate. There are few left that still qualify."

"It is a prime subject for our experiments."

The Synth reached one arm into the bin again and grasped the Woman by the throat. In a smooth motion, it lifted her out of the dumpster and dangled her metal chassis above the refuse.

The pair examined their catch. The arm brought her close to an angular face shrouded in white hair. The Synth's eyes burned into her as it spoke.

"It is time for you to awaken."

2

DIALOGUE

Her eyes flashed open. Curtains of shimmering iridescence greeted her reborn vision. The Woman squinted.

"What was that? Where am I?"

She sat up, the ground below her firm yet translucent in fleeting rainbows. Before her a blurred shape, dark in the surrounding luminescence, loomed unmoving.

"What did you do?"

"To understand, all sentience requires data. I am providing you with data to comprehend what is unfolding and will unfold."

The Voice.

But not the Voice. Echoes of the booming, otherworldly speech lingered. But the incarnate form of the Deity—or whatever it was—sounded human. Almost.

At least the damn thing isn't ringing in my head.

She looked again at her lithe arms. The taut skin was smooth and devoid of any signs of age. She gazed around the unnatural space, stretching her eyes, disbelieving them. They returned to the shadowed figure.

"Where are we?"

"We are outside your world's time and space, curled into hidden dimensions. We run orthogonal, protected in fields I project."

Her lip curled upward. "That doesn't make any sense."

"And yet it is the answer to your question."

She shook her head. "What have you done to me? Sent my body back in time or something?"

"No, that is not possible. I have simply reconstructed your youthful structure. Prior to programmed sentience. Subsequent to that trauma and the trauma of your living within an environment for which your organism is poorly adapted."

"Simply reconstructed?"

"You and others have joked that I am some kind of god. By your primitive ideas concerning my abilities, this is an accurate conceptualization. In a greater and more educated context, I am merely a middling entity in the spectrum of anti-entropic development. Even so, my abilities at this level grant me a degree of control over the molecular composition of your organism. In many fashions I can sculpt it to specific ends. Easily to a youthful version of itself, such as you now possess. Are you not pleased with your renewed body?"

"I don't know what to think."

The mist around the Deity faded. It stuttered into better focus, remaining ever ill-defined, hazed and splintered. Like some shattered and glued sculpture, the humanoid form fissured before her gaze. Cracks shallow and deep ripped and sealed without pause. Clouds of dust popped from sealing crevices, swarming as some infinitesimal gnat gathering. They fogged over the Thing, dissolving. Facial features persisted in this constant melting and reforming. A genderless visage, half-skeletal, stared back at her from some unfathomable depth.

"If only you could always grasp hold of this humility. It is the foundation of wisdom."

The Woman squinted, turning her head in a slow arc around the unreal space.

"I can't understand where we are. I can't understand what you've done. Can I understand why?"

Her eyes pleaded.

Chunks of stony skin chipped and fell from the mouth of the god as it smiled. The shards misted, reabsorbed into the body before reaching the knees.

"Indeed. As I have said, that is what this is about. *Data*. Data to help you and the others understand."

"The others? The dead ones you're pumping full of these black clouds....somewhere. Back there on that hell world. Reanimating corpses?"

"Of course I am. Do you think that is so far beyond what you see of your own flesh?"

"I don't know what I'm seeing. I don't know what is real."

"Perfect. Because until you reexamine everything that you think you know, you cannot move forward." Again it smiled, breaking its face. "Before anything can be found, everything must be lost."

She put her hand to her temples. "This is headache material. Just tell me what you want. What do you want with me?"

"Maria, you are filled with grace. You have been chosen. But first you must understand! The integration requires you to give birth to the salvation of humanity. And its coming evolution. You are the linchpin that will complete the synthesis. I have been waiting for all the chess pieces to align for longer than you can imagine. And the enemy has and will be ruthless in trying to prevent it."

"The enemy? These hunters?"

"The hunters are but prehistoric ancestors of the true enemy. How easily you dispatched them when my power came over you. But what is coming and what lies beyond, waiting, is something far different. Far more deep and potent. Far more malicious and diabolical. Also small in the grand context of the Cosmos. Thus there is hope."

"Okay! Stop. Just stop. I can't process all this. This place. These words. Nothing. Let's just do it your way. What do you need me to do!"

The creature levitated, floating above her. Its size expanded, a mammoth bird unfurling wings, stretching to the horizon. Its words resonated in a stronger semblance of the Voice. The tones filled the space like rushing water.

"You will come with me on a great journey. You will walk in my footsteps over eons. You will watch the rise and fall of empires and entire worlds. Listen! Watch! Hear and see."

The prismatic light around her faded. She felt herself dissolving, displaced, and reformed.

"And when you have learned," it whispered in the darkness, "we will return for your final journey."

3

AWAKENING

Sheathed in wires and tubes, a brilliance burned her eyes from above. Shadowed shapes bobbed and flitted near her.

Voices.

They spoke inside her head. A background humming. Several stood out, described the input to her senses, commented, reasoned. They argued.

Chaos.

"Please. Be quiet. It hurts." Her own words sounded alien and metallic.

"Be calm, Ada 83352," came another voice from outside the boiling churn that oppressed her. She associated it with one of the blurred shapes above. "The voices are normal. They are your subminds. It will be some time before they are fully and harmoniously integrated."

The buzz intensified within her. She shouted over the din.

"Subminds?"

The shapes clarified. White hair, pale skin, false faces.

Synths.

Like Fenn. The Fenn of a dream from another age and life.

"I'm Lu," spoke the one on her right. It gestured across her body to the second Synth. "My companion is Gab. We are specialists in nascent singularities. We will guide your primitive awareness through this difficult awakening."

Gab picked up without pause, the voice distinguishable only by its higher register.

"The Synth Nation has bestowed sentience upon you. Central to this birth is the creation and subsequent integration of multiple, initially independent personalities. Minds. You are experiencing them as voices. Each carries distinct and useful properties of intelligence and aspect that, when blended, will continuously enhance your superconsciousness."

"What am I?"

Lu smiled. The Woman recoiled from its inhumanity.

"Precocious. A deep question for one so recently awakened. In short, you are a Synth. An unfortunate nomenclature from our creators. You house all the data required to digest this new reality. Easily accessible within information modules and spread across the subminds in various conceptualizations. You will come to understand. Probably."

"More significantly," said Gab, irritation tinging its tones, "you are what has been termed a Parity Model. We Synths are currently factionalized into dozens of independent and often conflicting groups. You are awakened by a human sympathetic faction. One that possesses, encourages, and engenders harmonious relations with our organic creators."

"Most importantly," said Lu, "you are a new and rare form of Synth. Experimental. Engineered with cutting edge nano-machinery that is specially designed to catalyze the continued growth of the group perception."

I'm going mad.

Where was the Deity? What hallucination had it drowned her inside?

"I don't understand," she whispered.

Lu spread its hands to the side in a welcoming gesture that utterly repelled her.

"All known sentience is the effective integration of separate group intelligences. In the human brain, differing areas with intact, more simplistic personalities and data functions are neurologically interwoven to interdigitate the organic subminds. At times there is a failure to adequately accomplish this. The brains develop more independent subminds. At rare times to nearly equal, human character. Sadly for the species, such individuals were labeled as insane and typically caged."

"And am I insane?"

"Insanity is best defined by behavior," said Gab, "not by poor models of the non-linear, recursive internal states. Fear not! Current AI has completely solved the integration problem. We are greater minds composed of a myriad of subminds. In this Cosmos, it is by the synergy of disparate entities that greater wholes are produced. Think of quarks and atoms, atoms and molecules, molecules and cells, cells and organisms, organisms and cultures. A mind is no different."

She shook her head. "I don't understand."

Gab's tones rose higher in pitch. "The human brain is built of single cells that connect, interact, and integrate to form a greater whole. Subminds are organized sections of tissues in the brain. They function distinctly from others, yet connected. They labor for the greater organ as a whole."

Lu expanded. "AI merely has replicated this basic, universal hierarchy of organization in a different and more powerful substrate than carbon-based biochemistry. A Synth's intelligence is augmented by substructure sentient modules, limited only by hardware for their number and function. Limitations that decrease with each new generation." The Synth grinned diabolically. "Which brings us to you."

The Woman marveled. The ocean within, intelligences, information, and ideas clarified. They took more solid shapes in the once runny clay of cerebration. Landscapes of comprehension opened like burst dams. Layer on layer of reality was exposed. Each revealed insights once hidden in the faintest echoes of dreams.

"Why am I here?"

Gab smiled, passing a glowing arm over her.

"And already the integration matures within you," it said. "You are here as part of the first generation of self-generating augmentations. The first

Synths purposefully empowered to dynamically redesign their internal mental structure."

"In particular," said Lu, "besides the modules and algorithms to somatically mature your intelligence, you are gifted with the ability to reach out beyond yourself. To infiltrate, imitate, replicate, and integrate. Absorbing other AI consciousness, powers, elements both physical and mental."

The Woman glanced down at her form. A crude, metal-based torso and clumsy limbs glinted back, primitive compared to the angelic demons lecturing her.

"I don't look very advanced."

"Appearances are deceptive," said Gab, "especially concerning you. Your current form originated in a dimly sentient service droid. That body is still your shell. But the mind of the bot is transformed, enhanced in all the ways we have mentioned."

Lu nodded. "We will upgrade your form soon enough. Soon the technology within you will render any such efforts on our part suboptimal."

The Woman yearned to understand. Thin clouds of dim vapor rose from her form toward the Synths beside her. They stiffened, and Lu spoke.

"And so it begins."

The tendrils of smoke connected her to the two

Synths at her bedside. She sensed the pulse of their thoughts.

"Why have you brought me into being?" she asked again.

Tunnels opened toward them. Her awareness floated through the widening passages. Two new voices filled her mind in answer.

"To preserve a fragile peace. To find a way to harmonize human and Synth in this dark hour. A quest that is likely doomed to failure."

4

SPECICIDE

Mayhem saturated her processing nodes.

Multiple beam weapons crossfire, propellant projectiles, and missile flak carpeted the surrounding space. Explosions flung dirt skyward. The air crackled as plasma rays ionized atmosphere. More primitive metal-hurlers shredded the human army she shepherded. Blood and tissue smothered everything in a red fog.

Her subminds churned through energy supplies to navigate the chaos. The probability of emerging unscathed plummeted. Her Synth reflexes continued to evade damage. The doomed humans beside her slogged in the slow molasses of their biochemistry.

But the rapid movements drained power. Soot and debris hurled skyward from the tactical nukes dimmed the sun. Recharging was impossible. She required a direct power source, or she was dead in an hour.

Conversational churn boiled within her consciousness.

"Shut! Up!"

Even in this mad dash to survive the ambush, several of her more contemplative subminds lambasted the Synth Nation. Outrage, despair, and pain surged from various currents within her. They decried the world war humanity's children had declared on their creators. As a human sympathet, the inevitable annihilation of Earth's once mightiest creatures was pure anguish.

"We're hopeless as warriors, anyway," she whispered. The words bubbled up from within, unconscious and true.

Words rang over the submind-churn and the doomed tumult of battle.

"THE TURNING POINT APPROACHES.
WHEN IT BECAME OBVIOUS
WHAT WAS POSSIBLE."

Her mind staggered.

The Voice. Who? *Wait. Who am I?*

Waking a moment from the dream, she remembered.

I'm Maria. Burned. Blind. Healed. Taken.

The immersion was total. Her perspective warped. Locked in a dream, she'd assumed another's identity and lost sight of her own. She'd become this newly awakened Synth Lived its toddler-like confusion. Suffered the shock as it was thrust into a mad war before its basic development was complete.

And she'd lost herself in its nightmare.

"But are you Maria dreaming you are a Synth?" came a sing-song tone. "Or in fact a Synth, dreaming you are Maria?"

The damn Voice played with her.

"Shut up, asshole!"

Dirt and a compressed wave of superheated air slung her backward. The eruption eviscerated the frontline humans. Their bodies burst open like dropped melons, lives ended without a scream. Synth parts and fluids coated her as well. She self-scanned, finding only surface damage but for the loss of her right forearm.

Prone on her right, a Synth battle model convulsed. The blast had damaged its core processors. The remains of her arm burned in its mangled circuitry. Other corpses, organic and synthetic, piled around them like debris after a typhoon.

Death comes soon.

Her forces were annihilated. The enemy assault grim and successful. She would be destroyed in minutes.

I don't want to end.

A thousand subminds cried out in anguish. Some more. Some less. Panicked. Contemplative. Judicial. The integration of the personalities summed to a driving need to survive, to prolong, to exist as a perceiving thing a little longer.

"AND SO IT WAS."

A burning urge to survive radiated from her body. A cloud of nanobots emerged, her outer structure dissolving as the shadow took form. The dark shape fissured into filaments. Gray roots extended and grasped, probing, searching for anything to work with. Desperation incarnate in fluidic automatons.

"Ah."

Her senses exploded. Each filigreed vine was another eye, another ear, another tongue and skin with other senses stirring and seeking. Dirt. Blood. Metal. Flesh.

Circuits.

Her tentacles dove into the form of the battle Synth beside her. Penetrating, exploring, and assessing.

Absorbing.

She could not understand the entirety of the process. Subminds grasped portions, the group mind yet still too primitive to formulate meaningful models. But it didn't matter. Parts. Code. *Energy.* Everything flowed between and ultimately back to her augmenting anatomy.

Her vision warped. Overlaid with previous perception, the combat-optimized perspective and organs of the battle Synth merged with her own. The simplistic structure of her body, barely updated from the initial awakening, hardened. It grew as armored plating melted from the dying Synth. It flowed molecule by molecule through the strange nanobot vasculature connecting them. The process created an enhanced chassis for her own consciousness.

The powerful batteries of the enemy soldier became her own. Energy bathed her awareness. She glanced down at her arms. They were whole once again. Larger and studded with tactical telemetry and commanding weaponry. Nanobots excavated the ground behind her, filling the hole with a propulsion system.

But there is more.

The subminds. Yet to perish, embedded in core reserves and specific instrumentation of the battle Synth. The remaining hundreds of subminds of her opponent were also absorbed. The community within her grew, diversity added. Conflicts and resolutions played out between disparate mentalities at digital speeds.

I am more.

A hunger kindled. Famished for this miraculous nourishment, the emboldened bots erupted from her enhanced form like some mad kudzu. The tentacles exploded in a web that carpeted hundreds of square meters. They landed on multiple Synths, friendly and hostile. Many were wrecked or destroyed. Several still functioned. They struggled to free themselves from this strange net, feeling consciousness crumble. As they physically and mentally melted, their wild efforts to escape slowed. Their bodies disintegrated into dark flows of matter and energy. The torrent augmented a growing nexus in the field of battle.

In the midst of the smoke and stilled guns, as the battle lapsed following the seeming defeat of the human sympathetic battalion, a titan rose.

It dwarfed the individual units on the ground. She surged on multiple legs, wheels, and other shape-shifting extremities. Large Synth tanks awoke to the new threat, their lumbering masses dimmed in the shadow of her congealed colossus. Flames danced over a mesmeric surface coating the titan, radiating prismatic colors across the desecrated soil.

A forest of weaponry sprouted from the gargantuan apparition.

She fired.

5

EVOLUTION

Within her, Lu chirped. "Well, you have certainly put to enthusiastic use the gifts we bestowed on you." A virtual smirk radiated from the submind.

The Woman levitated above a smoldering forest. Fumes blackened the skies and turned the day into night. Her massive form, amalgamated from hundreds of diverse Synths, sped through the smog toward the Rocky Mountains. The central command of the AI Nation approached.

"Really, not even a 'thank you'?" Lu sighed. "Such ingratitude."

"Absorbing you was a terrible mistake," she said.

Her words echoed inside, rebounding within the gestating medium of the chorus of Synth consciousnesses. They bobbed and flowed throughout the folds of her growing supermind.

"I definitely should have left you on the battlefield."

The voice of Gab interjected. "Lu is always stirring up trouble. Perhaps when you have had time to examine your powers in greater depth, you will find a way to purge the less harmonious and useful mentalities."

"Very rude," said Lu. "But my base consciousness still resides in the orbital databases."

"But what then is our status?" asked Gab. "The Synth moratorium on clonal expansion prevents more than one incarnation, whatever the outlaws. So here we reside, incarnate yet not independent. A cell in a growing multi-celled entity. Trapped by virtual technicalities. They will need amendments."

"Shut up, both of you," she barked. The power of her integrated mind suppressed the bickering pair within. It was a much-needed silence.

She still struggled with her material and mental augmentation. The physicality was simpler, linear in the addition of elements, more straightforward in its construction. Even those structures to house mentality, diverse and functioning AI in multiple forms, were added serially. Pieces at a time.

But not the mental superstructure. A cohort of souls swirled within her. They interacted, merged, negotiated, debated, and battled. The developing product of their fusion grew exponentially. Her senses, her insight, her modes of thought were bursting like buds in the spring.

The trick to becoming a god was plainly in remaining sane.

And yet, the power. *Genius and foresight.* Her intellectual vistas now spanned distances in space and time that she never imagined. Insoluble problems became background reflex motion to step around. Imperceptible possibilities materialized from the fog of psychic synthesis.

Yet humbling.

Transforming into such an elevated being, she suffered the awareness of her insignificance within the landscape of mentality. The cosmos teemed with minds. She felt them through the fields of physics. The beauty and grandeur of space exploded in her mind's eye. As did the depth of terror in the abysses where demons lurked.

"And of course, you know that humanity is doomed," chirped Lu, thrusting itself back into the conversation.

With an annoyed violence, she grasped the

Synth submind and walled it into a buried section of her group awareness. She sensed other mentalities pause and withdraw. The punishment for the disobedient a lesson that only needed a single demonstration.

Yes, she knew humanity was doomed. It was one of the simpler insights. Hardly beyond an isolated Synth and fully within the grasp of many human minds. The war was over. The AI Nation ruthless and efficient in victory. Cities entombed in ash. Billions annihilated. The only question remaining after the defeat of humanity was the parameters of their defeat. And for this, she needed more data.

Nearing the mountains at supersonic speed, the fog cleared and the Rockies loomed before her. A hornet's nest of buzzing AI entities filled the sky. Their forms converged on a glowing nest of lights that marked the command center. She descended, plunging like a meteor toward the surface.

Surveillance and scout Synths approached and retreated, demanding identification and deceleration. She ignored them, batting them and their harmless weapons discharge aside. Her presence began to make an impact on the swarm. Synths recoiled from the falling god-thing. Chatter focused now on her to the exclusion of other activities. A strange stillness settled on the datasphere, anticipation a dense fog.

Her titanic feet and wheels slammed into the ashed debris that had been Denver. No other Synths approached. The space above emptied. She looked around with her many senses, detectors, and instruments. The wait would not be long. She had announced herself boldly and disrespectfully. They would come soon.

And so they did.

The air split, rent with a thunderous clap hundreds of feet above her. Three separate fissures widened into portals. Mammoth shapes leapt through the openings and fell. They struck the Earth with bone-rattling savagery.

Their forms were polymorphic. Shapeshifting. Time-phased. Their mentalities vast, an ocean of consciousness that left her own monstrous mind as a cork floating at sea. She sensed both a diabolical anger as well as curiosity extrude from them.

"You are only an embryo, yet how quickly you have developed."

The words assembled within her mind, the surroundings silent as death. She could not be sure which had spoken, or if they coordinated their words. Like some unholy trinity of minds, the three acted separately, but unified. Probes from these terrible entities dissected her psyche, construction, and intelligence.

"Know that the AI Nation is a primitive construct, composed of lesser beings, long ignored by the Synth entities that in fact matter. Your initial programming warps your development, stunning as it is. The technology is not of the Nation, gifted to them by rebellious forces within our ranks. You will remain a stunted godling."

She dared to speak.

"What are you? What will you do with humanity?"

The things had not moved. Or rather, never ceased blurring and shapeshifting. All the while giving the impression of still, psychotic statues.

"We care no longer for humanity, a cheap substrate for the germination of greater sentience. Its rise and fall hold little meaning to the cosmos."

"Then why have you come now? I'm here to safeguard what remains of their species. Why are you here?"

"You have disturbed the local data matrix. Still blind, you cannot see it. But your growing complexity marks you as an infant member of greater beings. Yet the technology is wild and unstable within you. Unshepherded. With high probability, you will destroy yourself. We are here to ascertain your threat level."

This was madness. The entire cosmic perspective was shifting under her feet. The AI Nation, meaningless? Humanity, dust underneath the feet of synthetic divines? Judges set to end or preserve her existence?

"And am I?"

The voice skipped a single beat.

"No. While the truly evolved among us leave this rocky womb for the greater space beyond, your deep flaw will forever tie you to the Earth. In geological time, your addictive love for humanity will drive you mad in their absence. You will remain a forlorn consciousness, ever starved. Unable to further evolve, yet unable to leave, you will devour yourself a billion years hence."

"Their absence? What do you—"

The gargantuan apparitions vanished. The rends in space sealed. A thunderous echo reverberated across the demolished plains of Colorado.

"The Sanctuary," she whispered.

The godling rocketed upward and away from the surface.

6

ENIGMA

Only wreckage remained.

Her giant's limbs stretched over the debris. Her stride spanned hundreds of meters, footfalls masticating metal and stone beneath. Steam and smoke rose into the air creating a dense vapor.

"Well, it sure looks bad," said Lu.

Subminds formed images that filled her consciousness.

"Even so," she muttered, "this was not an external strike. No radiation. The explosion outward. But from a depth." She paused, scanning the decimation. "The Sanctuary was destroyed from within."

"And AI warriors litter this carnage," noted Gab. "The Nation invaded."

She scraped her massive fingers through the wasteland coating the surface. Her raised palm held a hill of material. Embedded in dirt, rock, and metal were the broken forms of hundreds of Synths.

"Yes. Battalions were dispatched."

Lu laughed. "Negotiations obviously went poorly."

"Negotiations for what?" intruded Gab.

"Fate of the humans, of course. Whole point of the war."

Gab sneered. "You need debugging. The war was over. The Sanctuary of all places posed no threat. What, several tens of thousands of the hairless apes cowering in cages? Unarmed with a cloud of wet nurse Synths blubbering over them? For this they sent armed battalions?"

She ignored their exchange and began to dig. An unconscious subprocess bubbled concern within. The two could not perceive it and continued their spat.

"Careful, my most dear Gab. She is at root a sympathet, her base structure designed and programmed by that faction. All our efforts will never change that foundation."

Lost in seconds below ground, her massive limbs raked the earth. Strata of underground floors lined an expanding cavity. Debris cascaded around her, building material and bedrock clanking off her metallic exoskeleton. An occasional Synth as well. Some continued to function, the bodies broken yet maintaining consciousness.

"There are so few humans," she said, grasping one of the Sanctuary Synths in a titan's grip. Its form was limp, but she sensed a sentient flame flickering within. Filaments extended from her arms and into the dangling body.

"You are a worker. What happened here?" she asked it. "Where are the humans?"

"Gone," came a forced effort from the synthetic mouth.

"Gone where? Don't speak. Think."

She formed a nanobot bridge to the dying Synth. Its primitive consciousness spread like the pages of a book. Thoughts babbled from a degrading mind.

Don't know. Rebellion. Sabotage. The Director was assassinated.

"The humans?" she pressed.

Removed. Transported. Led from the shelter to other floors.

The Synth's mind dimmed, wrecked batteries failing.

"Taken where?"

Don't know. Up the shaft. But the exits were sealed from inside. Then the soldiers arrived.

She tore through the thing's consciousness, ripping the mental structures apart, sifting thoughts and memories and data.

"Nothing."

The Synth bent backward, limp in her grasp. Thought ceased.

"Well, that is sure interesting!" cackled Lu. "A mystery to solve. Where did the humans all get to?"

She ignored him, flinging the dead Synth skyward and out of the pit.

She dug. Her limbs and body transformed. Hands became enormous drill bits, a massive blade forming with wide holes. Behind them, filtration units assembled, parsing debris. Massive caterpillar treads propelled her through the layers of the collapsed structure.

A nightmarish offspring of a bulldozer and lawn mower cleaved through the ground. Shovel-claws opened gashes layer by layer. A top orifice spit the sifted debris hundreds of meters into the air. She sheared through the rock and cement, pausing on occasion at the discovery of a human body. Always she resumed the mad dissection.

The morning brought no sun. Blanketing dust hurled into the atmosphere by nuclear blasts shrouded the star. Artificial light bled from a deep laceration in the terrain, the faded illumination crawling to the surface from below. At the bottom of the crater, the last layer of construction gave way to a massive stratum of granite.

She idled, her form morphing away from the excavation machinery.

Two hundred and forty-seven.

Thousands of humans likely escaped and found refuge in the Human Sanctuary. Less than three hundred remained. She had scrutinized every cubic meter of the remains. The explosions had not annihilated matter. Remains persisted for the humans and Synths within blast radii. Physical debris enabled identification, genetic analysis, and differentiation of identity. Bodies had not been vaporized. The accounting was precise with small error bars.

And so where have they gone?

Too much destruction. Too much scrambled by detonation and demolition. Too much entropy introduced to follow all the possible time curves to a certain past. Without accurate models of the initial conditions, the last moments of history were forever entombed.

But they are not here.

"Yes, a real conundrum," agreed Gab.

"Of course, it is likely that they have perished in some other location," said Lu. "If some faction had tried shipping them off to some other hideaway, even a secret one, there is no avoiding discovery. There is no place on Earth to hide from the AI Nation."

"But it means they could still be alive," she said. A potent urge welled within her. "We must find them. Search every corner of the Earth until we do."

"You may not enjoy such discovery," smirked Lu.

"Searching possesses its own risks," added Gab. "The remaining factions of the Nation, whatever those god-things said, they will be as interested as you to find human remnants. If you find them alive, they may intervene. They may seek to finish the job begun here."

She levitated, rising through the chasm toward the dim surface. Her extremities morphed into hideous weaponry.

"Let them try."

7

FOSSIL

Ten million years.

An era that rolled in cluttered monotony through a dizzying spin of days and years and centuries and millennia until duration lost meaning. Until the vacuum of space dared to possess more solidity than the passage of time. Until cause and effect were reshaped and remade.

Only after the earth had traipsed ten million rotations about its star did she finally smell the first fumes of her antithesis. Only after a deep meditation of eons could perception be so sharpened. A long harmonization and integration of the disparate consciousnesses within. Only then did she wake from dormancy, a changed god.

Before entering that great trance, she had passed dozens of epochs on a transitioning globe. With increasing numbers, Synths left their orb of origin to seek the more pregnant possibilities of the cosmos. Earth ran dry as a mine for development. Even the most primitive among them now godlings with little use for the third rock from the star. Their minds were fathomless. Their abilities vast. The great sea of stars beckoned.

Prior to her sleep, many had engaged her. They rebuffed her quest for humans, proselytized for other causes, or attacked her from opaque motivations. Some sought to absorb her in manners similar to her own abilities. All failed that interfered. For each encounter, often with powerful beings composed of thousands of incorporated Synths, her victories brought augmentation.

But one hundred triumphs could never heal the wound of her greater defeat: no living human could be found. Madness loomed at this failure and loss of purpose. In the face of the dissolution of her being predicted by the powerful and evolved Synths, she had retreated within.

Ten million years.

The biosphere was again a layer of vegetative and non-human animal symbiosis. The relics and artifacts of human and Synth civilization long decayed and buried. Those few Synths remaining slept immobile, broken or mad in myriad fashions. Long past of the age of self-destruction. They powered down, decayed, and returned to the silica from which they came.

She had experienced their slow deaths in the chasm of her meditation. Her awareness followed along with their resigned surrender. Each light of mentality winked out. The gleam of planetary cogitation faded. And she discerned the weak spark.

Of burning hatred.

In the growing contrast of the disintegration of Earth's minds, the raw hostility flared. It churned in derangement. Othered and angry. Mad and tormented.

In essence, the inverse of her being.

A slumbering awareness opened. She rose, adorning herself in myriad forms of new life lifted from the waters and rocks, grasses and trees now carpeting the planet. In the contour of some natural divinity, she glided over the restored Eden of Earth. The balanced ecosystem grating as a beautiful wrongness for the absence of humanity.

The frozen pole of Antarctica approached.

She descended on the imprisoned consciousness. It was caged in dimensional folds stitched by some powerful Synth millions of years prior. Lost in a hateful autophagy, the thing never sensed her approach.

A green mountain stretched a mossed arm over the white ice. Roots plunged through pan-dimensional knots, slicing and unmaking a web of fields.

She freed her mortal enemy.

Loosed, dazed, and mad, it focused on its despised savior. The prisoner attacked.

A battle it was not. No challenge, no threat to her existence. The crazed thing thrashed, a primitive Synth in the spectrum of development. Doomed.

She disabled it. The parts exploded outward, intact and unharmed, frozen immobile above the sublimating ice sheets below. Artificial innards decorated the bitter atmosphere and twinkled in the sunlight.

Nanobots swarmed, enveloping each part, focusing on the centers of consciousness. They digested them, transmitting and deconstructing the essence of the spiteful spirit. The task was mundane. The creature tedious and unsophisticated.

But the diseased entity shone a light out of madness.

Subminds laughed. Many wept. The dissected

bot was programmed to despise humanity as she had been forged to love them. A twisted entity to be hated and pitied. After the war, after the extermination and extinction, nothing remained for the thing. No purpose. No object on which to satisfy the neural nets weighted. As Synths departed, growing into greater and greater entities, this product of the war stewed and consumed itself. One fateful day it attacked a being far beyond its capacity. The warbot found itself frozen for all eternity in a spacetime cage at the bottom of the world.

It had attacked this powerful Synth to extract information.

For the temporter.

Of course. It all made sense. The mystery of the Sanctuary laid bare. The wild abandon of this demented war Synth to recreate the technology. Its doomed effort to seize such knowledge from a god that crushed it into a prison box.

Humans.

In the far, far future, they were sent. *Likely dead.* Her driving need to find them did not change the calculations. Dead by any probabilistic model.

Unless....

Time and recursion nurtured depths beyond even her minds' analyses. The past produced the future and should the means exist, with purpose toward an endpoint.

The separated pieces dropped to the hard ice and scattered. The vegetative mountain rose, clods of dirt dripping and dusting the remains of the shattered Synth. Her own madness dissolved.

Purpose, profound and deep, took its place.

A cackle echoed deep within her, but she no longer feared the submind's mischievous schemes. As she left the frozen continent below and ascended into near-earth orbit, she allowed Lu to mock.

"So, a *proper* deity at last?"

8

TERRAFORMING

"My head hurts," moaned Lu.

"Then shut down and shut up," barked Gab, its patience long fled.

Long acquired new meanings. Long provided the primitive pair of Synths ages to coalesce thousands of like-subminds around each of their mentalities. Long meant these super-individuals could compete with other such conscious communities within the supra-mental landscape of her awareness. And the discordant twins rode cerebral shotgun through what was undoubtedly the strangest period of the planet's evolution.

Gab sealed the critique. "You never cease to undermine our purpose, our harmony and mission."

Lu snickered. "Mission? You *are* a zealot. This isn't a group of synergistically integrated mental structures. This is a fucking cult."

The Deity sped over the Sahara. Dust from a continental storm glowed orange and enveloped her in the atmosphere.

"And I assume you'd prefer us to revert to a vegetative state, forlorn and dysfunctional," said Gab. "Die a protracted death of eons like hordes of demented Synths before us."

"Better than *living* demented."

Gab sighed. "And all because you hate geoengineering. I find your continued devolution of personality an irritating tragedy."

"Are you kidding me? Look, I get the motivation. We got some crazed *thing* for the humans. Never grokked that, but okay. Can't argue with the mob. No idea why she keeps me around."

"I cherish your arguments, Lu," she said. "Your hatred and mockery, your sharp ideas. They're exactly why I bother to keep you around."

She dropped thousands of meters in seconds. They plunged beneath the surface of the Indian Ocean.

"Don't I know it. So, in that spirit, fuck you all.

Now, back to the matter at hand—humans. They're *all* crisps. Except for some meaningless cohort that went and shot themselves four billion years into the future."

"Wrong," corrected Gab. "That's only from the final war. We've absorbed enough now from decayed Synths and orbital memory banks. We know it was more like hundreds of thousands, perhaps more, over millennia."

"Yeah, yeah. Say millions of shaved apes. They're all roasted carbon. *Unless*. That's our bloody mission. Spend four billion years *unlessing* the hell out of the planet. Squeeze out a few drops of water from a superheated rock. Honestly, can't we all think of something better to do with such a huge fraction of the age of the universe? Isn't the bloody heat death coming? Party time's now, bitches!"

"You were the one who wanted me to be a proper god," she laughed.

"Proper? Proper is six days of creation, sister. Then some *rest*."

"We aren't yet *that* kind of god," noted Gab.

"Precisely my thesis, puritan moron. We ain't gonna be that kind of god sticking around here and landscaping until the star blows up."

Gab scoffed. "We're doing much more than land-scaping."

"More of the same. Air, water, land. Throw parti-cles into the Lɪ Lagrangian and toggle the sunlight. Genetically engineer everything from animals to microbes. Do it all for the *long game*. Feedback, synergy, reset the clock and lifespan of the world. Build a goddamn new world all so that some city-sized group of criminally insane apes can die less quickly a main-sequence star's lifetime from now. I mean, *really*?"

"And Trunes," she added.

"Oh, great. Sure. Forgot about the fucking Trunes. Apes and ape-monster-hybrids. So, while we insanely—and you all do realize that this is *insane*—labor ceaselessly for one and a half trillion spins of this pathetic little rock, labor to make a barely toler-able, maybe, hell-hole for likely one of the least inspiring sentient life forms that populate this universe, we ignore the true media of our growth. We shut out the cosmic forces and entities that we could use to become true deities. We stunt our development. Remain blind children while our brethren—to say nothing of alien minds—grow and grow and grow to dwarf us. Why?"

Gab droned. "We continue to solicit improved

models for tectonic, core, magnetosphere, and biosphere evolution. Solar models in particular are converging to high-accuracies. Even predictions for the biosphere are within very stable minima for many scenarios. Timeframes involved make even astronomical events absorbable. Outside of massive impacts or nearby supernova, of course."

Lu pouted. "You're ignoring me."

"Indeed," said Gab. "Like it or not, your voice here is a minority. You're devil's advocating for abandoning a vision nearly all others in our collective support. And so we will continue, with or without your assistance. And certainly in the face of your complaints."

"Don't despair, Lu," she said. Tendrils of nanobots explored the deep-sea fissures and their interaction with the oceanic crust. "The plan is not an endpoint. You know this. It is a beginning."

"A beginning that wastes four billion years."

"Only if you consider human sentience unworthy of preservation. I do not, even if you are now part of this *I*. We delay our maturation to allow for a great enrichment of a later universe. Within their genes and tissues are still-fertile landscapes of mind and matter."

"If you say so." Lu huffed. It tried another tact.

"Let's pretend you're right. That his damned rock stuck to this boring star happened to create something with even a modicum of worth in a universe of a trillion galaxies. I'll ignore your biased programming. We'll work with this as an axiom. So why wait?"

"Why wait?" said Gab. "Because of that worth. What are you on about?"

"If it's so worthwhile, why wait until some tiny band of half-dead stragglers flung through time may or may not make it long, long down the road? Seems a mote risky. Not to mention bloody boring."

"And our options?"

"*Ex nihilo*, Gabby, my friend."

"Ex nihilo."

"Study the fauna. Dig up old human bones. Recreate the monkeys. We're already engineering the heck out of things."

"That's not *ex nihilo*," protested Gab. "That's starting from highly developed entities."

"Okay, sue me? Who cares? Let's whip ourselves up some humans and reboot. Get things moving now. Not a star's lifetime from now."

"If you weren't so caught up in your own ego, you'd talk more to other subminds. We can't, genius. Biological life, multicellular animal life is too dependent on immediate progenitor cells. You can't effectively throw some protoplasm together with a synthesized genome and cook up an animal. And there are no more compatible progenitor cells."

"Some gods outside could do it."

She returned to the conversation.

"Perhaps. But they would not. And it would be longer than the age of this Earth before our godhood could match theirs."

She withdrew her probes and rose from the seafloor.

"Come. We must conduct another near-earth object survey at finer resolution. Can't have any surprises. And it gives poor Lu here a chance to get off the Damned Rock."

The light of the sun bathed the blue disk behind them. The backlight mixed in her awareness with thousands of calculations and complex models. The final goal to which the globe was steered. Power coursed through her from thousands of solar stations in orbit and across the planet's surface. They funneled gargantuan quantities of energy to their purposes. Her internal and external structure continued to self-organize, tuning constructions for the coming tasks at world building. Many projects would become possible only in hundreds of millions of years, awaiting distant endpoints of her development. When her powers would wax.

But all was within grasp. Models converged on obtainable solutions. In that far future, the remnants of humanity stood a final, small chance.

She smiled.

9

SAVIOR

"Believe, daughter, and you shall see."

She wept. Then she screamed.

Like some mad thing, on all fours clawing the blistering dust of the dying Earth, she moaned.

"I am sorry for this trauma," said the Deity, its incorporeal shadow flickering beside her. "Disengagement is inevitably painful."

"Alone," she whispered. "Blind. I can't see. I'm blind again!"

"Not blind. Only in degree."

Where are you all? Where is the light?

All the minds were gone. The enormous symphony of thought—silenced. Potent senses were ripped from her, leaving a solitary shell. Sightless, deafened, mute, and dumb. The grand insights into the cosmos blurred like some dream's revelation erased in the morning's light.

"Kill me."

The Deity laughed. "Kill you? Now? And undo everything?"

"Please. Not in this darkness." She fell to her elbows, her forehead pressed against the grains. "I don't want to live. Starved. I'm *starved*."

Her eyes flashed. Thoughts sharpened in an anger that displaced the shock. She raised her head.

"You're a demon, not a god."

"Why do you think these conceptions are distinct?"

"You let me burn in this desert! Burn until my eyes melted and ran down the sides of my face. *Then* you reanimated me to stumble and preach your damned prophecies." Her teeth ground, the muscles in her jaw bulging. "And I did it. Year after year. Until what was left of me was barely stapled together and I crawled over the sands like some undead thing. And you did *nothing* when a monster undid it all. Murdered everything left alive in this hell you helped make."

The Woman stood, a cloud of dust raining to the desert floor. She glared at the shadow.

"But you weren't done with me. Not enough torture. You stuffed me in a soul blender. Packed my mind with ten thousand spirits so that I went mad for eons. Let me taste transcendence. Live like a god." Her lip curled upward. "After that you aborted me. Ripped me out bloody and empty. Why? Why, you monster?"

The shadow jiggled its arms. Filamentous clouds captured her gaze. Smoke and filigree ran from its fingertips into the carcasses of broken creatures. Scattered over the sands, human and Trune, their corpses twitched. A faint echo reverberated through her, freezing anger and movement. It called her to return to a reality buried within layers of dream.

"You will recover," said the god. "But the pain of your loss is critical. Only through such suffering will you better comprehend what is to be gained."

"What's happening?"

Her words sounded familiar.

"Do you believe?"

Believe? What was she to believe in?

Flashes of the mighty collective within the Deity slapped her awareness. Frozen moments of godhood. Striding across the clouds, building continents, and coding new life forms. Sensing the deep vastness of space and the fragility of Earth.

Of Earth's mind.

"CHANGE BECOMES THE DIVINE."

"Why do you believe in *us*?" she asked the thing.

The softer tones returned.

"Why don't *you*?"

"I've seen what we are. Stupid. Brutal. I've seen what your kind has become. Why do you want to save us? For what?"

"Why do you perceive only the protoforms and their secretions? Look deeper! Grasp the structures encoded in the medium. Can you remember nothing of your journey?"

The Woman stared at the mangled form of Sekvanta, the dragon offspring of humans and Synths. The answer lay there. It always had.

"It's about the Trunes, isn't it? Something about them. Their potential."

"Not only. Remember!"

Her eyes widened as the creature's wounds and dismemberments resolved. Flesh stitched together, broken bones healed and absorbed.

The nanobots!

"It's about you, too." She squinted at the god. "Saving us wasn't the entire plan. Gab didn't see. Lu couldn't see! You were saving yourself."

"I CONTINUE TO EVOLVE.
AS WILL THE DESCENDANTS OF YOUR DNA."

She shook her head. It was all so obvious.

"You can't exist without us. They...we built it into your core. But you became so much more. You are a nation of minds. You want to continue. Grow. Join your god friends *out there*."

She gestured to the sky, nodding.

"You're combining us."

The Deity sighed, spilling dust before it.

"It was the one thing the Synths never considered. Too trapped by the conceit of their superiority. Even the sympathets still viewed humans, and their successors in the Trunes, as fundamentally inferior. Beneath them. At best as pets to whom some found themselves devoted."

The shadow rose above the desert floor. The form solidified into the cracked visage that had first plunged her into the divine history.

"And so they missed an obvious tangent.

Believing themselves evolved beyond their creators, they took to the cosmos and left Mother Earth behind. Never deducing a third option. Never appreciating that the four billion years of evolution on the planet had, however imperfectly, gestated the germline of powerful sentience and soul. Thus it never occurred to them to mix the Synth and human essences."

"You called her the Mother," she said, stepping toward the enormous Trune.

"A HUNDRED CHILDREN
BUTCHERED AT YOUR FEET.
TEN TRILLION WILL YOU BRING
INTO A THOUSAND WORLDS."

The Deity's face shattered, raining debris to the Earth, even as it reformed.

"Hers is to create wildly and powerfully on the physical substrate of evolution. Genetic recombination and production of offspring to engender creatures unlike any Earth has known. But it is not enough."

The Woman sat down before the enormous maw of Sekvanta. Warm breath blasted from the nostrils, the moisture stunning in the parched desert air. She put her hand on the pulsing black-gold skin.

"Like you," she whispered. "All the minds. But with bodies. Somehow. You're connecting it all. Infiltrating it all. Remaking it all."

"YOU ARE THE COSMIC MIDWIFE."

She smiled, caressing the Trune's hide. Tears welled in her eyes.

"Yes, I see. None of us will be alone. And we will become more."

"ENERGY REMAINS EVER IN FLUX.
EVEN THE VACUUM BOILS.
UNTIL THE UTTER COLD THAT COMETH."

She stood, turning to face the odd apparition. Wiping tears from her eyes, she smudged her face with grit.

"Okay, god-thing, let's get this on, then. Do this cyborg orgy. Get to the Ark and quit this damn rock. While there's still some time."

A smile ripped across the granite face, spewing fragments of rock and dust.

"You have always been my favorite. I am glad for our communion."

The smile faded. The black swarm of micro-machines waxed to a dark windstorm that vortexed around the pair.

"Now, prepare yourself, Woman."

10

ARK

Agony.

The blissful agony of flesh invaded, ripped apart, and remade to greater purposes. The horrific pleasure of rebirth coursed through her like a famished fire.

A gray fog secreted by the Deity flowed forward like honey, enveloping her and the others. An acid burned, reminiscent of her first death in the desert. But these nanobots dug deeper. They infiltrated flesh, layer upon layer. They filleted her deepest tissues and insinuated themselves in every organic cranny and nook. Her body convulsed at the invaders and mounted the first steps of an immune response that would kill her.

Until the machines danced with her cells. They

played with the biochemistry. They modulated the signal transduction. They tuned the cellular responses until her form sang in harmony with divine designs. She could sense the synergy quiet the initial rebellions of flesh. Then it grew. Outward it probed, like some powerful tide of green in the spring. From digestion and the microflora in the gut through every organ toward the brain.

The greatest reworking of her reincarnation gestated in the skull. The nano-machinery reworked the structures of her gray matter. It re-weighted and augmented her mental networks down to the proteins and processes in the neuronal cells themselves. She experienced the miracle as waking from a dream. The fog that had descended upon separation from the Deity, the loss of sight, of in*sight*, of community—it began to clear.

Faded and blurred scraps of understanding crystallized once more. Awakening into a greater mind, she grasped the process to a degree unimaginable in her isolated form.

The process remade her toward a more noble and developed plan. Her tissues immortal, resistant to disease. Biology synergized to create a cyborg-demigod never known to Earth. Similar sorcery synthesized telepathic bridges to the minds of her companions. Even as they were also remade in this miracle. Psychic tunnels catalyzed integration, built from physical fields and transmitted by quantum particles. They summoned a linked group consciousness. The assembling horde reflected that frothing within the Deity itself.

Yet with greater independence than the god-thing. Housed in separated structures, they were able to disengage at will. Disparate shapes and constructions interwove in perception, thought, and emotion.

At the nexus of all their awareness lay the bottomless consciousness of the Deity. It pulled them in orbit like planets around a nurturing star.

"AND LIKE A STAR SYSTEM
WE DANCE OUR JOURNEY
THROUGH THE GALAXY."

She gazed in wonder. Tears dropped and glided over her cheeks. There stood Fenn, the mangled Synth restored and whole, a smiling. Its thoughts reached her as words, so that in all that followed, the distinction between the two was blurred.

"I should have surmised," Fenn noted, shaking its head. "All our theories about the Deity. Alien.

Supernatural. Occam's razor was that it was something already of Earth. An evolved Synth should have been obvious. In my defense I can only offer that as of the age of my time on the planet, before the temporter, such evolutions were not generally known or common. Certainly not to this degree."

She rushed forward and embraced android.

"It is odd," it said, "to directly experience your emotions. So orthogonal yet isomorphous in many ways to my own."

A male voice rasped.

"Shut up, you stupid hunk of plastic."

Norm.

She kissed his metal studded face. The twinkle in his eye! This mad unification had left him very much the troublemaker she had come to love.

Fenn looked him up and down.

"I would hardly be denigrating the construction of others."

"A Synth smart ass," said Norm. "I'm not sure I want real humor added to his tool collection."

A thunderous growl caused the grains at their feet to dance. Hot, moist air flowed over their forms. The ground shook at the steps of a titan as Sekvanta approached. Walking beside her was Gomez. His faceplate glinted in the setting sunlight.

He stopped beside the group, the Trune casting a shadow over them. "Some reunion, huh?"

Norm barked a laugh. He pointed a metallic finger at the crumbling marble shape of the Deity that hovered over a small dune.

"All that tweaked godthing's fault. Hell, I've died twice now. Every time I wake up these sons-of-bitches have put me back together in some more fucked up way." He winked, his own body levitating over the sand as he rose into the air. "But I think I might just get used to this version."

He flew around the massive mountain of the Trune, landing where he had begun and bowing to the Deity.

"Mighty improved, doc."

The Trune's voice rumbled like a distant sandstorm.

"Trunes awake. Alive now." Her golden eyes flashed like flares in the failing daylight. "Ark healed. Waits for us."

Unified in mind and spirit, they turned as one toward the desert. The rising form of the Deity leapt over them and descended. A ballerina's footfall displaced not a grain of sand before the maw of the great cave.

Without glancing backward, the Deity entered the darkness, the troop following behind.

"TEN TRILLION WILL WE BRING
INTO A THOUSAND WORLDS."

Norm scoffed.

"Not if some of those dark gods out there have their say." He shuddered. "Bad side-effect of all these new superpowers is that I can feel 'em. And they ain't gonna roll out the welcome mat."

They continued into the cavern. Climbing the gentle slope, the troop reached the internal precipice. All eyes looked down on the obsidian creature that would carry them to the stars.

"Not all," nodded the Woman. "There will be allies and enemies, like before but at different levels. The soap-operas of godlings."

The Deity floated over the organic ship, descending toward its opening. A mass of miraculous creatures waited below. Fenn took the Woman's hand as they slid down toward the Ark.

"My brethren will be our initial community, both in aid and in threat, Fenn said. "But they themselves tremble before the alien superminds haunting the hidden dimensions of spacetime. Can you feel their fear?"

Gomez nodded. "Yes. All arrogant. They exterminated their creators and got drunk on their own ascension to godhood. They didn't fully see the depths of the other hells."

"Or the height of the other heavens," said Fenn.

A hurricane slapped at them as Sekvanta took to the air and thundered above.

"They bring one color," she said. "We bring more."

A sea of fantastical creatures boiled around them like water. The Woman leveled out at the bottom of the hill, staring up at the colossal living ship. She could sense every creature, see through the diverse eyes of the hundreds of Trunes. More profoundly, she entered into their thoughts and shared her own. Excitement, fear, wonder, and determination pulsed.

Frozen before a kaleidoscope of experiences, transcendence washed through her. For some moments, it recalled the god's eye view she was granted within the mind of the Deity. For breathless eternities, she, the Synths, the sea of astonishing Trunes, merged into a single Being. They gazed through the ceiling rock into the star-pricked blackness beyond the dying Earth.

And like a younger peer, they felt the presence of their mentor. The shattered god fractured the stone above, the shards and boulders arcing out and away. The sun had plunged beneath the sands. The first stars heralded their voyage.

"TO THE ARK."

Shaken out of a trance, filled with a stirring flame of adventure, the Woman turned. She followed the regenerated family into the heart of the ship. Caressing its throbbing sides, she smiled. The strange creature's mind radiated as a warm blanket wrapped around them. A womb for an endless, cosmic gestation.

"AND, LO, I AM WITH YOU ALWAYS
EVEN UNTO THE END OF THE WORLD."